KATIE MORAG
and the WEDDING

Grannie's

The Mainland

The New Pier

The Jetty

ISLE of STRUAY
SHOP & POST OFFICE

OBAN
TIMES
GET
YOUR COPY
HERE

BISTRO

TO THE
NEW PIER

CRAFTS

WELCOME

WEST
HIGHLAND
FREE PRESS

ORDER
NOW

The Shop & Post Office

ALSO BY MAIRI HEDDERWICK IN RED FOX

Katie Morag and the New Pier
Katie Morag and the Two Grandmothers
Katie Morag and the Big Boy Cousins
Katie Morag and the Grand Concert
Katie Morag Delivers the Mail
Katie Morag and the Tiresome Ted
Katie Morag and the Riddles
Katie Morag's Rainy Day Book
The Big Katie Morag Storybook
The Second Katie Morag Storybook

A Red Fox Book

Published by Random House Children's Books
20 Vauxhall Bridge Road, London SW1V 2SA

A division of The Random House Group Ltd
London Melbourne Sydney Auckland
Johannesburg and agencies throughout the world

Copyright © Mairi Hedderwick 1995

7 9 10 8 6

First published in Great Britain
by The Bodley Head Children's Books 1995
Red Fox edition 1997

Printed in Hong Kong

THE RANDOM HOUSE GROUP Limited Reg. No. 954009

ISBN 0 09 946341 5

Katie Morag
and the Wedding

Mairi Hedderwick

Wedding invitation

The Pleasure of the Company of

The McColls

is requested

RED FOX

Ever since the new pier had been built on the Isle of Struay, Granma Mainland visited regularly.

Katie Morag McColl was delighted to see more of her other grandmother. But most delighted of all the islanders was Neilly Beag. He fancied Granma Mainland and always looked so sad when she went away. Then he would write lots of long letters to her in the city on the mainland and wait impatiently for the mailboat to bring back a reply.

This kept Mrs McColl, the Postmistress, very busy. Everyone on the island said a romance was afoot.

"Maybe even a wedding!" whispered the Ferryman's wife in between serving teas to the visitors.

"Pah! A wedding? I'll believe it when I see it!" muttered Grannie Island when she heard the gossip.

Katie Morag was very excited at the thought of a wedding. It usually meant a big party; it also meant that the two people getting married wanted to live together instead of far apart.

Would Granma Mainland come to live in Neilly Beag's house on the island? That would be lovely! But, oh dear, what if Neilly went to live with Granma Mainland in the far away city?

"If there is a wedding will Neilly Beag be our Grandad?" Katie Morag asked when she and Liam arrived at Grannie Island's, just in time for dinner.

Her Grannie did not answer.

"Wheesht! Go sit at the table!" she frowned instead.

"We've got two grandmothers. Why don't we have two grandfathers?"

"Wheesht! Will you SIT DOWN!" glared Grannie Island.

It was a long time since Katie Morag had seen such a glower in Grannie Island's eye. It was time to stop asking questions.

OLD PHOTOS

As Katie Morag pushed Liam homewards she wondered why Grannie Island was in such a bad mood. It made her feel sad.

When they got to the village Neilly Beag was at his front door. He had a huge pile of stamped addressed envelopes in his arms.

"The invitations for the wedding!" he beamed proudly. "Can you take them to the Post Office, Katie Morag?"

That cheered Katie Morag up no end.

"Can *we* go? Can *we* go?" chorused Katie Morag and Liam when the silver and gold invitation was put on the mantelpiece.

"Of course!" smiled Mr and Mrs McColl. "*Everyone* will be going to the wedding!"

"And the new baby?"

"Of course . . ."

"And the Ferryman and his wife . . . and the Lady Artist . . . and the new teacher?"

"Of course! Of course!" laughed Mr and Mrs McColl.

"And Grannie Island?" asked Katie Morag.

Suddenly everything went very quiet in the McColl kitchen. Grown ups can be very strange thought Katie Morag, sometimes they answer questions and sometimes they do not . . .

That night in bed Katie Morag complained to Liam.

"If we didn't answer when we were asked questions we would be called rude."

"Rood!" agreed Liam.

KATIE MORAG & THE NEW PIER
KATIE MORAG & THE BIG BOY COUSINS
KATIE MORAG & THE TIRESOME TED
KATIE MORAG & THE TWO GRANDMOTHERS
KATIE MORAG DELIVERS THE MAIL

MAY
M T W T F S Sun

"Granma Mainland always answers questions. I am going to write her a letter," declared Katie Morag.

This is what the letter said:

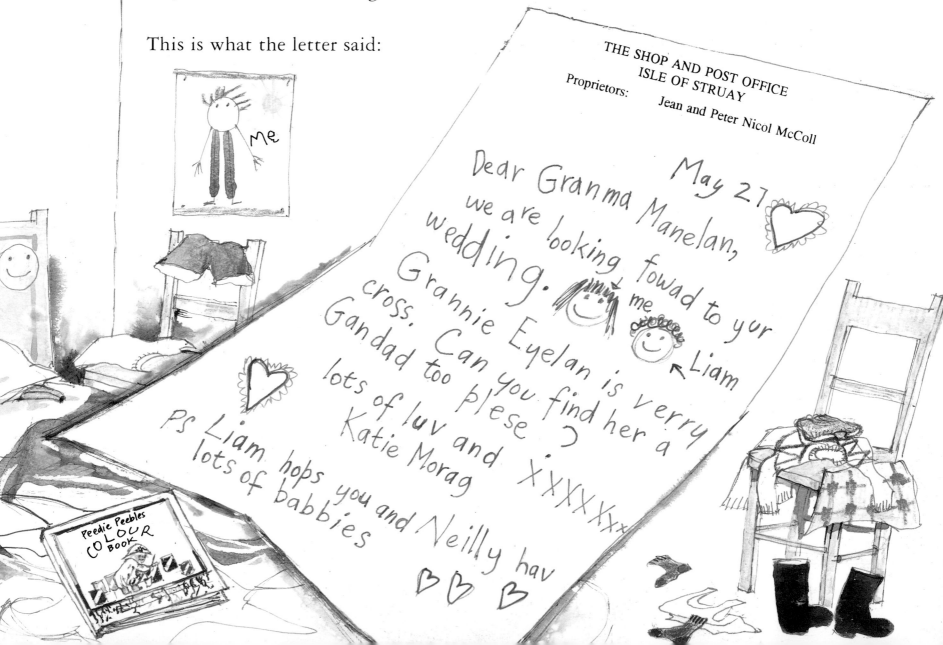

THE SHOP AND POST OFFICE
ISLE OF STRUAY
Proprietors: Jean and Peter Nicol McColl

Me

May 27

Dear Granma Manelan,
we are looking fowad to yur
wedding. me
Grannie Eyelan is verry
cross. Can you find her a
Gandad too plese?
lots of luv and
Katie Morag XXXXXx
PS Liam hops you and Neilly hav
lots of babbies

← Liam

Peedie Peebles COLOUR BOOK

The next few weeks on the island were very busy.

All sorts of parcels and crates came off the boat and were carried up to Neilly's house or to the Village Hall.

Neilly dieted so much Mrs McColl had to get a needle and thread to alter his smart new suit. The Ferryman's wife made a giant of a chocolate cake; she and Mr McColl had to stand on stools to decorate it.

BULK ICING SUGAR

COCOA

Katie Morag and Liam made a special present for the bride and groom.
The new baby lent ribbons for flags. Liam thought it was Christmas. He
kept chanting "Anta Claws! Anta Claws!" and even hung up his stocking.
Katie Morag waited for a reply from Granma Mainland.

The day of the wedding drew near.

Granma Mainland and all the relatives and friends were due to arrive on the boat the day before the big event.

Nobody had seen Grannie Island for days.

The speech sign in the helicopter reads:

I'VE FOUND HIM!

All the islanders went to the pier to meet the guests arriving off the boat, but there was *no* sign of Granma Mainland. Neilly Beag was just about to burst into tears when a loud clattering and whirring reverberated around Village Bay.

It was a helicopter and Granma Mainland was right in the front with the white bearded pilot.

"Anta Claws!" yelled Liam.

"It isn't Santa Claus, silly!" cried Katie Morag. *She* knew who it was.

Grandad Island swung Katie Morag up in the air. "Last time I saw you, Katie Morag, you were just a sparkle in your mum and dad's eyes!"

Katie Morag and Liam raced Grandad Island up to the Village Hall to help with the decorations for the wedding party.

Grandad Island asked if Grannie Island was going to the wedding.

"You'd better go and find out for yourself," said Granma Mainland, somewhat sternly.

STRUAY VILLAGE HALL

KEY AT MRS. BAYVIEW'S
ALWAYS
PLEASE RETURN

FLY
ME

Katie Morag watched Grandad Island set off on the long walk round to Grannie Island's house, on the other side of the bay. She worried that the fierce glare in Grannie Island's eye of late would frighten him away.

The
Wedding
Menu

LOBSTER CLAW SOUP
OR
STUFFED TURNIP

HAGGIS BURGERS
OR
CARROT STEAKS

CHIPS

CAKE & ICECREAM

Katie Morag need not have worried.

On the day of the wedding nobody's eyes were glaring – everyone's eyes were sparkling, especially the two grandads'. But Grannie Island's and Granma Mainland's were the brightest and sparkliest eyes of all.

Granma Mainland and Neilly Beag were to honeymoon on the neighbouring island of Fuay. There were no people on Fuay, only sheep, and they all belonged to Neilly.

"And all the lambs next spring will be yours, Mrs Beag, my wee Bobby Dazzler!"

Liam was right. Granma Mainland *was* going to have lots of babies to look after.

GOOD LUCK

Sheep Dip

JUST MARRIED

HASTE YE BACK

But Granma Mainland was not going to give up her flat in the city. She and Neilly would commute between Struay, Fuay and the mainland. And Katie Morag could visit whenever she wanted.

It took a lot of persuading to get Grannie Island up in the helicopter.
Grannie Island did not like travelling.

Grandad Island loved travelling and never stayed in one place for long.

"East, West, Home's Best!" insisted Grannie Island, clinging to her
seat like a limpet.

Katie Morag knew then, that Grandad Island would be leaving soon.

"Grandad, when you go travelling can I come too sometimes?"

"Certainly, Katie Morag – anywhere in the world."

Katie Morag was thrilled. She looked forward to visiting Fuay, the city on the mainland and now, anywhere in the world!

But it was good to know that Grannie Island would always be there on the Island of Struay when she got back home.

More Red Fox picture books
for you to enjoy

ELMER
by David McKee

MUMMY LAID AN EGG
by Babette Cole

RUNAWAY TRAIN
by Benedict Blathwayt

DOGGER
by Shirley Hughes

WHERE THE WILD THINGS ARE
by Maurice Sendak

OLD BEAR
by Jane Hissey

MISTER MAGNOLIA
by Quentin Blake

ALFIE GETS IN FIRST
by Shirley Hughes

OI! GET OFF OUR TRAIN
by John Burningham

GORGEOUS
by Caroline Castle and Sam Childs